MAYHEM

#3

VS. THE SUPER BULLY

BY *KARA WEST*   ILLUSTRATED BY *LEEZA HERNANDEZ*

LITTLE SIMON

New York   London   Toronto   Sydney   New Delhi

ABDOBOOKS.COM

Reinforced library bound edition published in 2021 by Spotlight, a division of ABDO, PO Box 398166, Minneapolis, Minnesota 55439. Spotlight produces high-quality reinforced library bound editions for schools and libraries. Published by agreement with Little Simon.

Printed in the United States of America, North Mankato, Minnesota.
092020   012021

**THIS BOOK CONTAINS
RECYCLED MATERIALS**

LITTLE SIMON
An imprint of Simon & Schuster Children's Publishing Division
1230 Avenue of the Americas, New York, New York 10020
First Little Simon hardcover edition May 2019
Copyright © 2019 by Simon & Schuster, Inc.
All rights reserved, including the right of reproduction in whole or in part in any form.
LITTLE SIMON is a registered trademark of Simon & Schuster, Inc., and associated colophon is a trademark of Simon & Schuster, Inc.

Library of Congress Control Number: 2020940796

Publisher's Cataloging-in-Publication Data

Names: West, Kara, author. | Hernandez, Leeza, illustrator.
Title: Mia Mayhem vs. the super bully / by Kara West; illustrated by Leeza Hernandez.
Description: Minneapolis, Minnesota : Spotlight, 2021. | Series: Mia Mayhem; #3
Summary: When a super bully accuses Mia of not belonging, she has to learn how to hold her ground.
Identifiers: ISBN 9781532147500 (lib. bdg.)
Subjects: LCSH: Friendship--Juvenile fiction. | Running--Juvenile fiction. | Bullying--Juvenile fiction. | Shadows--Juvenile fiction. | Superheroes--Juvenile fiction. | African Americans--Juvenile fiction. | Schools--Juvenile fiction.
Classification: DDC [Fic]--dc23

Spotlight
A Division of ABDO
abdobooks.com

CONTENTS

CHAPTER 1

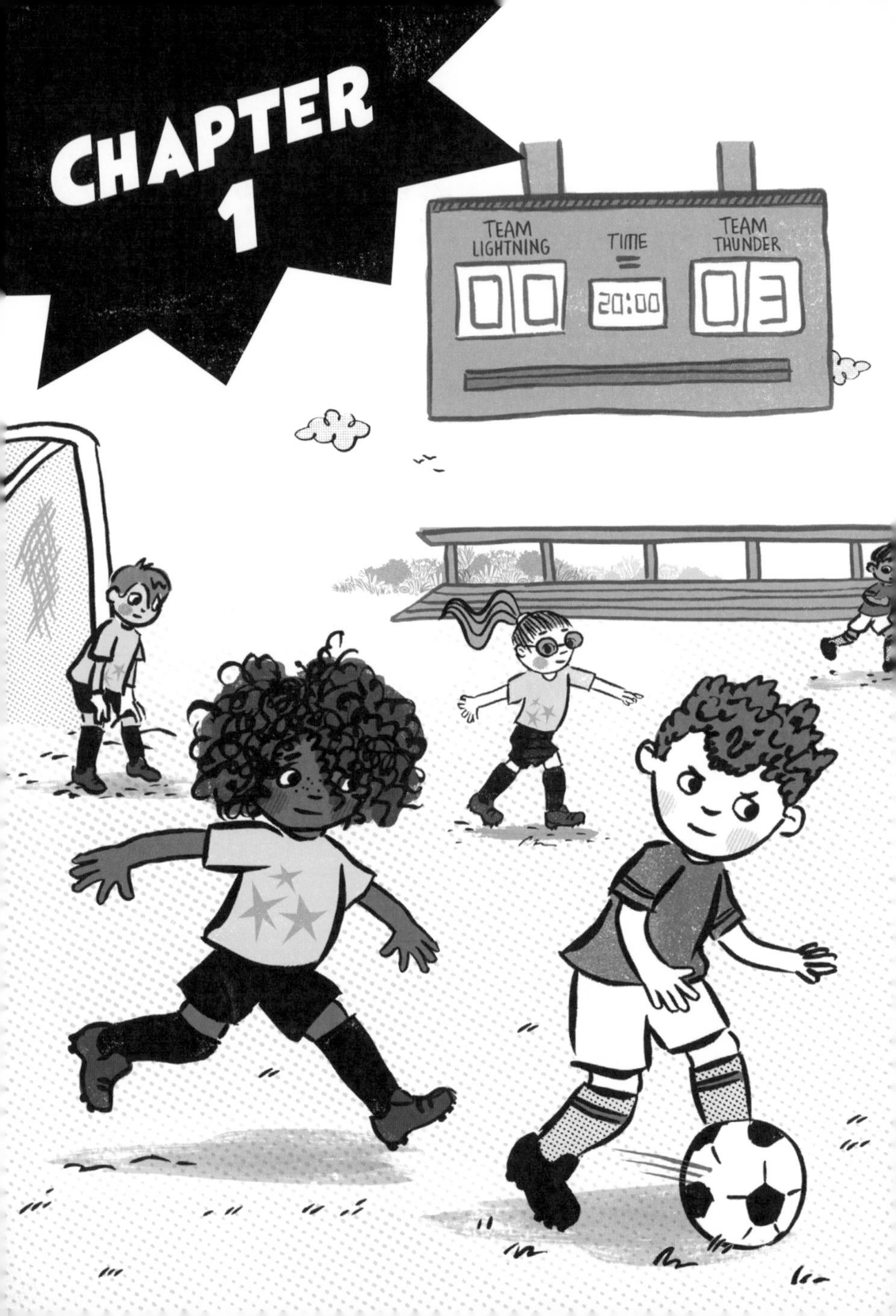

MIA MACAROONEY, THE SOCCER STAR!

Oh boy. We're totally going to lose this soccer game. I doubt we'll be able to make a comeback before time runs out. If by some miracle we do score a goal, *I* definitely need to stay out of it.

Why? Well, because the last time I was on this field, I kicked the ball so hard that I broke the goalpost by mistake!

1

Weird things happen to me all the time. In fact, all my life I thought I was a super-klutz. No matter how hard I tried to avoid it, I always caused a lot of mayhem.

But here's the kicker: I found out that I'm *not* a super-klutz. . . . I'm actually just SUPER!

Like for real!

I. Mia Macarooney. Am. A. Superhero!

Ever since I found out, I've had to juggle a lot. During the day, I go to Normal Elementary School. But as soon as the school bell rings, I head off to the Program for In Training Superheroes, aka the PITS. And at the PITS, I go by my superhero name, MIA MAYHEM!

My parents and my best friend are the only people who know the truth. Sometimes I wish I could tell everybody. But I've learned that keeping things quiet is the only way to protect my secret identity. My mom and dad would know best. They've been superheroes for *much* longer than me.

It's been a crazy ride, so I'm glad that I still do a lot of ordinary things like playing soccer with my friends. But now that I'm in the middle of a losing game, I'm starting to panic.

My best friend, Eddie, is about to pass the ball to me!

Oh boy. Here
we go.

"Run, Mia! Run!"
he yells as he
throws me the ball.

So I zigzagged my way around the
other team and ran the ball all the way
down the field . . . and kicked it straight
into the goal!

By the end of the game, I scored ten goals all by myself—without even breaking a sweat!

I ran over to my teammates with the biggest grin on my face. For the first time ever, we totally beat the odds . . . thanks to me!

Now, I kind of wished everybody could have been happier for me. But for some reason, all my teammates were too tired. They didn't even care that we won!

This wasn't exactly how I hoped to finish the best game of my life, but I guess it was okay.

I've got something else to look forward to.

Today is my very first superspeed training class at the PITS.

And I have a feeling it's going to be awesome.

CHAPTER
2

DO NOT
ENTER

MEETING ALLIE OOMPH

At the entrance to the PITS, I took out my suit. Then I spun around three times. I finally mastered the quick-superhero-change trick!

On the outside, the PITS looks like an empty, old warehouse. There's even a DO NOT ENTER sign dangling on the front. But when you walk in, it's a top secret superhero training school!

I looked around the lobby, which was known as the Compass. A group of older students walked by. I stopped a tall, slender girl in a violet suit. Maybe she would know where Dr. Dash's Fast class was.

"Oh sure!" she said, pointing to the back exit. "Fast class is outside. You need to go to the Super Cutie."

"To the super . . . *what*?" I asked, confused. But when I turned around, she was already gone.

Did she really just say "the Super Cutie"? That didn't sound right.

I walked in the direction she'd pointed, toward a big, arched door.

Maybe I needed to ask somebody else.

But then I'd have to ask if they'd seen the Super Cutie.

Um, yeah. No, thanks.

I opened the door and walked down a long tree-lined path. There was a clear, protective dome over the tall trees. Soon I saw a familiar blazing red cape up ahead.

"Hey, Penn!" I shouted excitedly, running to catch up.

When Penn Powers and I first met, we didn't exactly get off on the right foot. I thought he was a major show-off.

17

But luckily, we became friends after going on a flying mission to find my crazy cat.

We stood in front of a screen that looked like a robot. There were five superpower icons.

"Wow, even I've never been out here," said Penn.

I pointed at the picture that looked like three forward arrows. "Looks like Fast class is to the right," I said.

Just as we made the turn, someone knocked us down!

"Get out of the way, slowpokes!" the kid yelled, before he rushed on.

"Whoa. Are you guys okay?" asked a girl who ran over to help us up.

The girl was wearing a green supersuit that had silver zigzags on the elbows.

"Yeah, thanks," I replied. Then I bent down to brush the dirt off my boots.

"Whoa—your silver leg blades are awesome!" I exclaimed, looking up. Starting from the base of the knee, each of her lower legs was made of metal. Then at the ankle, a curved blade completed each foot. They fit perfectly with her blazing green suit.

"Yeah, aren't they cool?" she asked with a grin. "I call these my Blades of Glory! I've got all different kinds of legs depending on what I'm doing.

ALLIE'S KICKS

BUNGEE BLADES

ROCKET BLADES

These ones are great for running, so it's perfect for Fast class. Are you going there too?"

I nodded, and then Penn and I introduced ourselves.

"Nice to meet you! I'm Allie Oomph," she said warmly.

Once we got to the racetrack, there were many kids already there . . . including the rude kid who had knocked us over!

I wasn't too excited about that, but I didn't have time to worry.

Because out of nowhere, a swirl of wind blew past and pushed us over *again*.

This time, Penn fell onto me.

I fell onto Allie.

And Allie fell onto—uh-oh. It was the rude kid.

"Hey! Get off!" the boy said as he picked himself up.

Before we could say a word, the wind stopped. Then a man with a neat mustache and a golden whistle appeared in front of us.

"Sorry! Didn't mean to knock you all over. I'm Dr. Dash—welcome to your first Fast class!"

CHAPTER
3

QT ... **_NOT_**
CUTIE

Dr. Dash smiled. "Welcome, students. This is the hidden course called the Super Quick Track—or QT, for short."

Ha! So this is what the Super Cutie is! Penn gave me a thumbs-up.

"You will each learn how to control your speed by running around this beginner-level track," Dr. Dash continued.

The rude kid raised his hand. "This track looks *way* too easy. Can we skip ahead to a harder lesson?"

"Ah, Hugo Fast. It's good to see you," Dr. Dash replied. "The track may look easy now. But once you start running, hurdles will pop up everywhere."

POP!

Hugo didn't look happy, but he didn't argue.

"Now, let's cover the superspeed basics. Does anyone know what the most important rule is?" Dr. Dash asked.

Allie shot her hand up. "Remembering to stretch?"

"Good guess! It *is* important to relax your body." Dr. Dash smiled. "But the secret to becoming a good speedster is to take it slow and not go *too* fast. At least at first."

Everyone looked very confused.

"I know it doesn't quite make sense. But think of it this way," Dr. Dash began. "If you run several laps without preparing your body, you're going to run out of breath, right?"

Everybody nodded.

"Well, with superspeed, you can't push yourself before you're ready. If you do, you might lose your own *shadow*. And without your shadow, you'll lose your superspeed powers."

Everyone gasped, except for Hugo.

"Yes, it's very serious," Dr. Dash said. "Without your shadow, your body

will *literally* slow down. And finding a missing shadow is tricky business. Now, thankfully, there is a way to find it—but it's not something you'll need to learn now."

Whoa. Who knew your shadow could *leave* your body?

I wonder if it hurts. Well, actually, let's not think about that. I'm getting ahead of myself.

Once we finished covering the rules of speed, it was time to start a team relay race. My group included me, Penn, Allie . . . and, unfortunately, Hugo.

Each person had to run five laps while jumping over hurdles that popped up from the ground. As a penalty, every missed hurdle would be added to your team's overall time. And this combined score would be each team's final ranking for the race.

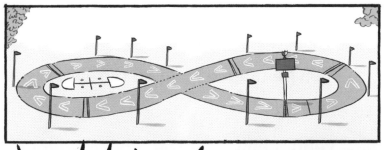

Talk about a lot of pressure, huh? But with Penn on my team, I was feeling pretty calm.

That is, until Hugo said he was taking charge. "That's the only way we'll actually place first," he insisted.

Then he tapped Penn on the shoulder to start.

"Penn Powers—I've heard your name before. Don't let me down," Hugo muttered.

Penn let out a half-hearted laugh as he and I locked eyes. Then he gave me a quick wink.

"On your marks!" Dr. Dash called out as the first group lined up. "Get set!"

WHEEEEP!

Penn leaned forward, his eyes focused straight ahead.

"Go!"

Dr. Dash blew his golden whistle, and Penn sped away.

THE RELAY RACE

All the starters ran off at the speed of light. A swirling blur of color that matched each runner's supersuit filled the lane. Allie and I cheered as Penn's bright red streak zoomed around.

Penn came into focus as his first hurdle popped up from the ground. Without missing a beat, he leaped into the air.

Whoa. Did you just see that?

He made it! And now he's in the lead!

From there, the first three laps were a piece of cake. Penn easily kept a large distance between him and the other runners. And things were looking really good . . . until a loud alarm started going off.

BEEP! **BEEP!** **BEEP!**

"Oh no!" I cried. "Penn's getting tired."

"I think everyone is," said Allie.

She was right. Beeping sounds were going off in every lane.

I watched with one eye half shut as Penn missed five hurdles in a row.

But the good news?

Thanks to his strong start, we were still in the lead.

The problem was that now it was *my* turn.

As Penn began his last lap, I stepped up to the start line and leaned forward. My muscles tightened as Penn's red blur came closer and closer. Then he tapped me in and off I went!

An awesome tingly feeling came over me. Right then I realized that I'd felt the same amazing rush during my soccer game earlier.

Soon, I could see my first set of hurdles coming up. I took a deep breath and jumped into the air. And leaped right over them!

From there, things were a piece of cake.

Well, at least until lap three.

By then, I ran out of all my energy— just like Penn.

I watched helplessly as a pink blur zoomed by on the right. Then a green streak edged past me on the left!

In an instant, we were in danger of losing our lead!

So I looked down and pounded my feet into the ground.

But looking down was a *bad* idea because my foot got caught on a long line of hurdles. And just like that, they all fell like dominos.

Then there was *a lot* of beeping.

But I still had to tag Allie in, so I ignored it and pushed to the end.

As soon as Allie blasted off, I dropped to the floor. It felt like the whole track was spinning! Luckily, things calmed down as Penn helped me up.

I checked the board at the back of the track.

Oh boy. Somehow, we were now in last place.

And I could tell Hugo was *not* happy about it.

CHAPTER 5

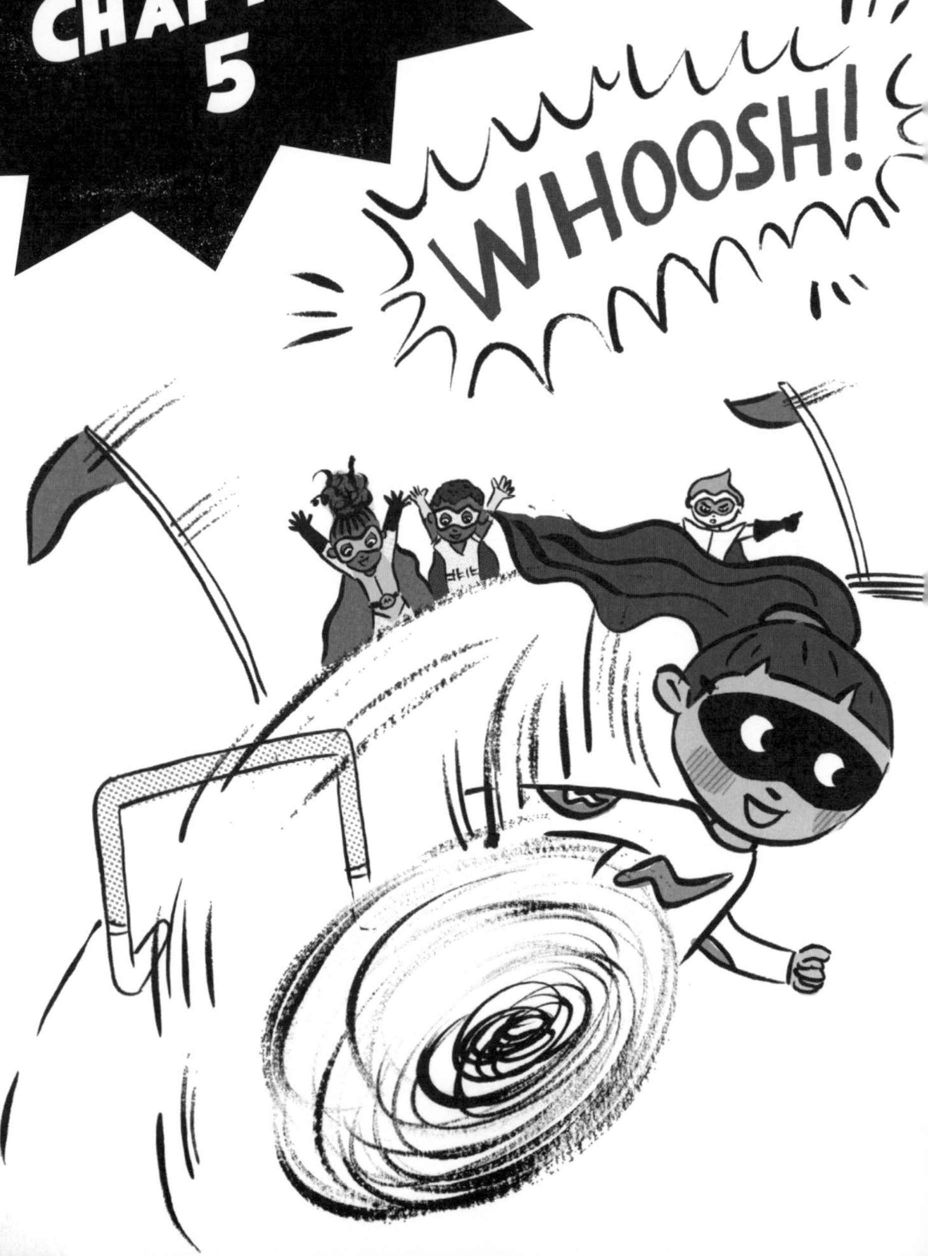

THE FINAL RESULTS

The QT race wasn't over yet, and the chances of making a comeback were slim. But Penn and I cheered at the tops of our lungs every time Allie passed by.

Hugo, on the other hand, wasn't a good cheerleader.

"Hey! You need to go faster!" he yelled as Allie came around a curve. "We're in last place!"

But Allie stayed focused and steady. Keeping her own pace.

And guess what?

It was the perfect plan.

Because by lap three, everyone else was pooped. And that's when she took her chance to get in front of a bunch of other kids.

55

When Allie tapped out, she was ten feet away from fourth place. She was also the only runner who hadn't missed a single hurdle!

Then it was Hugo's turn. He zoomed off in a bright orange streak.

I had to admit that as bossy as he was, he *was* a talented runner. He easily pushed forward and jumped over a string of moving hurdles.

In the end, Hugo got us up to second place.

For the first time during the whole race, I let out a sigh of relief.

"Great job, Allie! I'm so glad we made a comeback," I said.

"Thanks! I told you my blades were good for running," she replied.

"Yeah . . . well, they weren't fast enough," Hugo muttered as he walked by in a huff.

"Oh, don't listen to him," I assured her. "He's just tired."

She nodded with a bright smile.

Then Dr. Dash gathered the group. "Good job, class!" he cried. "You've finished your first race in record time.

But we need to tally up the missed
hurdles." After a long pause, he
announced the final scores. Then all
the color drained from my face.

Because we weren't in second.

We were still *last* . . . because of all the hurdles *I* missed!

"Ugh. Thanks a lot, Mia Mayhem," Hugo growled. "You undid all *my* work."

"No, it's okay, Mia," Allie said, patting me on the back. "This was a team effort. It's not your fault."

"Well, *you* ran like a slowpoke too.
Never mind your Blades of Glory.
They're more like Blades of GRASS!"
Hugo shot back.

"Ha! Well, actually my blades are made of metal. But maybe I should put green stripes on them! They'd match my suit," Allie replied with a big grin.

But Hugo tried again.

"Oh, that won't help. Because blades of grass *can't run*," Hugo said. "Like you."

Allie's smile didn't waver.

But I decided enough was enough.

"You know what, Hugo?" I said, jumping in. "Allie is not the problem. You are."

"No, I'm not. I'm the only one who actually *helped* the team. Even Penn messed up," he said, crossing his arms.

"Well, you sure aren't acting like a team member. Putting the blame on us just makes you a sore loser," I said.

"What did you say?" he asked as he got closer.

Penn tried to step in. But nothing was going to scare me—

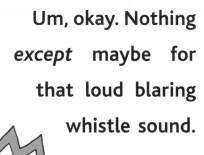 Um, okay. Nothing *except* maybe for that loud blaring whistle sound.

CHAPTER
6

THE LOST SHADOW

"Great job today, everyone!" Dr. Dash cried. "Class is dismissed. Make sure to get lots of rest for next week."

As the other kids left, I thought Hugo would make another snarky comeback. But I guess my plan worked because he just walked away.

"Don't worry about him," I said, turning to Allie.

"Oh, yeah, he doesn't bother me," she said. "He's just in a bad mood."

"Yeah, and it might never change," I said as we all laughed.

Then Penn, Allie, and I started the walk back to the PITS building. That's when another dizzy spell hit me. I steadied myself against a tree.

"What's wrong, Mia?" Penn asked as he came over.

"I don't know. I'm just a little dizzy," I replied.

"Oh no!" Dr. Dash suddenly chimed in from behind. "Mia, can I please see you for a moment? It won't take long."

So my friends left, and I followed Dr. Dash back to the track.

"Mia, would you please stand in sunlight?" he asked.

"Sure," I said as I walked out of the shade. My legs suddenly felt heavy.

"Oh, Mia," he said slowly. "I'm afraid what I'd warned about earlier has happened. You pushed your body too hard, and now your shadow is gone."

What? He couldn't be serious.

But I looked behind me . . . and he was right! My shadow had vamoosed!

"Oh no! It really is gone! Does that mean I've lost my superpowers?" I asked.

"Yes, your superspeed powers are gone," Dr. Dash said. "So your body will start to slow down. But don't worry."

"Are you sure?" I asked, trying to keep my voice steady.

"Yes, we'll have to start a special search, and—" he began.

But then a loud sound made us both jump.

Dr. Dash pulled his phone out of his pocket.

RING!

RING!

RING!

"Er—excuse me, Mia. This is a call I *have* to take."

So I waited patiently under a tree. And when he came back, he looked really worried.

"Sorry. Where was I?" he asked as he scratched his eyebrow. "Being shadowless *will* be uncomfortable, but you just need to be careful," he said. "The bad news is that we have to put the search on hold. I've been called into a secret runaway-train operation!"

Okay, hold on. Did you hear that?

I know I'm in quite a pickle myself. But a runaway train? Now that I'm a superhero, I know an emergency when I hear one. So we agreed to put the search on hold, and I headed back to the PITS. Really slowly.

When I finally made it inside, Penn

and Allie were waiting for me. So I told them my shadow was missing, but Dr. Dash would help after taking care of a secret mission. Now, I wasn't too worried about the waiting . . . until a random note fell out of my locker.

It said:

Meet me on the QT in two days, if you DARE. One more race. Just you and me.

−HF

Oh boy. I don't know what I just walked into. But I have a feeling I should have never called Hugo a sore loser.

CHAPTER 7

THE BAD LUCK DAY

At regular school the next morning, I was back on the soccer field. But today, I was moving super-slowly and was in no mood to play.

"Oh no. Looks like it's going to rain, huh?" Eddie asked.

"Uh, yeah. Thanks, Captain Obvious," I shot back.

Okay. So I didn't mean to be rude.

But I didn't want to think about the weather.

When the whistle blew, I ran toward the ball. But I could barely walk! In fact, my legs wouldn't even move.

So, unlike last time, I was *not* Mia, the soccer star. I was Mia, the benchwarmer, who couldn't play.

After the game, Eddie came over to check on me.

But I couldn't tell him that I'd lost my shadow. It was too risky that others could hear. And I had bigger problems on my mind. So as soon as the bell rang, I left without saying goodbye.

At the PITS, I ran
into the one person
I didn't want to see.
Hugo Fast was standing in the middle
of the Compass. If he knew that I really
was a slowpoke now, he'd use it against
me. So I slowly turned around to leave.
But I bumped right into Allie and Penn
and landed right on my butt!

As my friends helped me up, I told them my plan. I couldn't wait for Dr. Dash. The search had to start now.

And since a team was faster than doing it alone, we decided to split up outside. Penn flew over the trees but found nothing, while Allie turned over heavy, fallen tree trunks.

As for me? I had no choice but to trail behind. And tell them where to look.

"Hey, Mia! I found something!" Allie
called out excitedly.

Please, please, please be my shadow,
I thought.

She was pointing to a big black
circle on the ground.

I inched closer and poked it with my fingers. It was wet and super-shiny.

"Ugh. Since when do I look like a puddle?" I snapped as I fell in.

I knew Allie and Penn were trying to help. But this search was a total bust.

And I was now officially out of time.

At dinner that night, I told my parents about my day full of bad luck. My friends didn't understand, but my mom and dad would see it from my side. Or at least I thought they would.

"You have a bigger problem than your missing shadow," my mom said.

I looked at her, totally not following.

"Mia, losing your shadow makes things hard. But it'll come back," my dad explained.

My mom nodded. "I know there's a lot going on, but it sounds like you've been pretty mean. Always remember that it's hard to find good friends."

CHAPTER 8

SLOW AND STEADY

The next morning was another gray and gloomy day. After the last PITS dismissal bell, I was stretching on the QT when Hugo showed up.

"Wow, so you came," Hugo said. "I thought you would chicken out."

"No, I'm not a chicken," I replied.

"And *I* don't like being called a sore loser," Hugo snapped back.

So I actually *was* pretty nervous. But I needed to act cool. I wiped my sweaty hands at my sides.

"All right," Hugo said. "On my count, we're going to do twenty laps."

"What? Twenty laps!" I cried.

If I'd failed at five laps, how was I going to do twenty?

"Running the team relay race by ourselves is the only way to see who the real winner is," Hugo said with a smirk.

Now I really wanted to run away. But I knew I *literally* couldn't escape.

So there was only one option: I had to run the race . . . even if I lost horribly.

I took a deep breath and looked ahead. But then two figures flew down and landed right in front of us!

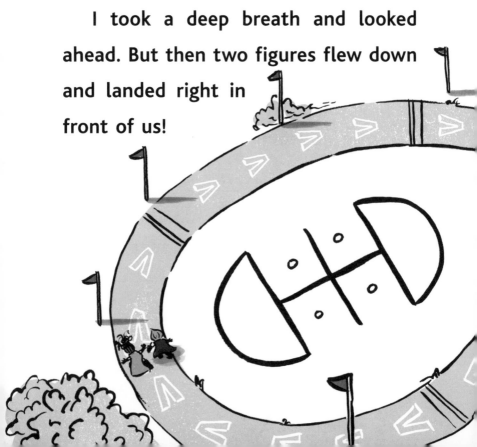

It was Allie and Penn. With pom-poms!

They gave me a wink and then ran over to the sidelines as Hugo started counting down.

ZOOM!

"Three . . . two . . . one. GO!" he yelled.

And just like that, the race was on. Hugo passed me five times before I even finished the first lap. I was going *super*-slow, but sweat still dripped down my face. I didn't even have blue-and-yellow sparks behind me! So I was feeling pretty down as I started my third lap.

"Mia, stay focused and steady!" Penn yelled from the sidelines.

"Yeah, and keep the pace!" Allie added.

Hearing her voice calmed me down. During the team race, Allie hadn't let Hugo bully her into going fast. And like Dr. Dash had said, pacing was the secret to superspeed!

I smiled and gave Allie a thumbs-up.

I was finally ready to finish this—whether I lost or not.

CHAPTER
9

CONNECTING THE PIECES

I was ten laps in when I realized it was starting to get easier.

I had no idea why. But like Dr. Dash told us, building speed was most important. Maybe while I was walking in the woods yesterday, I'd actually been preparing for today!

Whatever it was, I was definitely feeling better.

I felt a burst of speed and glanced behind me. The yellow and blue sparks were starting to come back!

As I rounded a curve, that's when I saw it.

A weird-shaped black blob was trailing behind me.

It looked like a person's hand . . . and then I realized it was a piece of my shadow!

I looked up at the sky. The big, dark clouds had finally parted. With the sunlight in my face, I kept on running as the black blob got bigger and bigger. Soon my full shadow was following behind me! I clenched my fists and realized they were totally dry. Who knew your shadow helped you from getting gross and sweaty!

With my body back up to speed, I easily sped around the track nine more times. Then finally, it was my last lap. I was trailing behind Hugo by just a few feet. I pushed as hard as I could, but Hugo passed the finish line first.

So, in the end, I lost again. But it was okay. I still felt great.

"Congratulations, Hugo," I said, catching my breath. "And I'm sorry I called you a sore loser."

"Yeah, whatever. But this time, I won fair and square," he said.

I nodded. Then Penn and Allie joined me, and Hugo left for the PITS.

"Oh, Mia, what a great race!" said a voice from behind.

I turned around and saw Dr. Dash.

"Sorry we couldn't find your shadow together, but it looks like you didn't need me!"

"It's because my friends helped me remember what was most important," I said, turning to Allie and Penn.

Then we all high-fived. And our shadows did too!

"One more thing," I said. "Sorry about snapping at you before. I was worried about finding my shadow, but that's no excuse for being a bad friend."

"That's okay," Penn said.

"Yeah, we understand," Allie said.

"Thanks, guys. You're the best," I said with a big smile. "But now that this race is over . . . the last one back to the PITS is a total slowpoke!"

CHAPTER
10

THE FINAL RACE

By the time we had our next class with Dr. Dash, I'd secretly been racing everywhere.

And good thing, too, because our next class was harder.

"All right, students! Today we're taking it to the next level! We'll have hurdles like before, but they will have an extra surprise."

Then he pushed a few buttons on his wristband. And all of a sudden, a whole group of superhero teachers landed in front of us, each with a brightly colored ball. One of the balls burst as Dr. Sue Perb landed, spraying water everywhere!

Oh boy. Giant water balloons!

"You'll also have to look out for us!" Dr. Dash cried excitedly. "Everybody, ready?"

Half of us cheered. Half of us groaned. And I was totally ready.

We were put into the same teams from before. As expected, Hugo wanted to take charge. And that was fine with me as long as I had my shadow.

Dr. Dash blew his whistle and soon, Allie was off! She wasn't the fastest, but she was steady and jumped over every hurdle and balloon!

Penn went second. He had trouble with the same hurdles as last time, but he still got us into first place.

Then it was my turn.

I started slowly, making sure I wasn't pushing too hard. Luckily, I was feeling strong, so I picked up speed. In the end, I avoided every single obstacle!

Then, like before, Hugo was the last runner on our team. His speed was good, but he couldn't focus on the hurdles and the balloons at the same time—so almost every single water balloon hit him. By the time he finished his final lap, he was soaking wet.

"Okay," Dr. Dash said at the end. "Time to calculate the number of missed hurdles per team."

We all held our breath and waited.

"Congratulations! The team in first place is Allie, Penn, Mia, and Hugo!"

We all cheered.

Allie tapped me on the back. "This is because of you! You ran so well and avoided every single hurdle!"

"Oh, it was a team effort!" I said. "And also, I actually owe a lot to Hugo. If he hadn't dared me to race him again the other day, I never would have done so well!"

Hugo just scowled as a trail of water followed behind him. "You just had some good luck today," he said. Then he walked away in a huff.

And you know what? He was right. I *was* lucky. But not the way he thought.

I was lucky to have great friends.

And I was even luckier that those friends knew how to be a good friend to me, even when I wasn't. Because after all, true friends support one another, even on the gloomiest of days. Just like Penn, Allie, and my best friend, Eddie.

That's when I realized I wasn't done with my apologies. I still owed one to him for being rude during our last soccer game!

There was so much to explain, and this apology couldn't wait for a single extra second.

But thank goodness I now know how to run superfast.

Bzzz!

119

KARA WEST

would love to be a superhero,
mostly so she could ask squirrels
what they're so nervous about.
She lives in Chicago with her own
cats, who, unlike Chaos, spend more
time sleeping than causing trouble.
Thank goodness.

LEEZA HERNANDEZ

has illustrated several books
for young readers including
New York Times bestselling
author John Lithgow's *Never Play
Music Right Next to the Zoo*.
Mia Mayhem is her first chapter
book series. When Leeza isn't
causing her own mayhem, she's
hiding in her art lair and drawing.
Her tabby sidekick, Jaspurrpurr, is
usually supernapping close by.
If Leeza were granted a superpower,
she'd speak and understand any
language in the galaxy.

COLLECT THEM ALL!

Set of 6 Hardcover Books ISBN: 978-1-5321-4747-0

Hardcover Book ISBN
978-1-5321-4748-7

Hardcover Book ISBN
978-1-5321-4749-4

Hardcover Book ISBN
978-1-5321-4750-0

Hardcover Book ISBN
978-1-5321-4751-7

Hardcover Book ISBN
978-1-5321-4752-4

Hardcover Book ISBN
978-1-5321-4753-1